P9-BYQ-627

To a small boy called Or and a smaller girl called Shir, with all my love.
And also with thanks to big kids Mandy, Libby, and Mike
for holding my hands all the way up the hill.

Copyright © 2014 by Yuval Zommer

All rights reserved. No part of this book may be reproduced, transmitted, or
stored in an information retrieval system in any form or by any means, graphic,
electronic, or mechanical, including photocopying, taping, and recording,
without prior written permission from the publisher.

First U.S. edition 2015

Library of Congress Catalog Card Number 2013955955
ISBN 978-0-7636-7403-8

14 15 16 17 18 19 TLF 10 9 8 7 6 5 4 3 2 1

Printed in Dongguan, Guangdong, China

This book was typeset in Aunt Mildred.
The illustrations were created digitally.

TEMPLAR BOOKS

an imprint of
Candlewick Press
99 Dover Street
Somerville, Massachusetts 02144
www.candlewick.com

THE BiG BLUE THiNG ON THE Hill

templar books
an imprint of Candlewick Press

SNO

ZZZZZZ

Far away from the city, in the middle of the Great Forest, was a special place called **HOWLING HILL**. During the day, it was peaceful and quiet because all the animals were asleep.

But at night, the forest really came **alive**. Out came the foxes and the weasels.

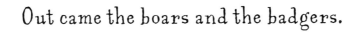

Out came the boars and the badgers.

The bears lumbered out of their lairs to practice their **growling.**

And the wolves crept out of their dens to practice their **HOWLING.**
All was well in the Great Forest at the foot of Howling Hill.
Until one night, when something **TERRIBLE** happened.

First there was a rumble,
then there was a ROAR,
and finally a terrifying sight appeared,
right on top of Howling Hill.

"It's a meteorite!" said the bears.
"It's a spaceship!" said the wolves.
"It's trouble!" said the foxes.
And the foxes were **right.**

So they all went to hide in the
Great Forest, hoping that the trouble
would soon be gone.

Early the next morning, the animals crept back to the foot
of Howling Hill, but the trouble was STILL there.

"It's a big blue elephant!" said the weasels
(who had never seen an elephant before).
"It's a big blue dinosaur!" said the
badgers (equally birdbrained).

"It's a **BIG BLUE THING,**" said the foxes (who were right again). And everyone agreed that it seemed to be awake and should probably be left alone until it fell asleep.

"Perhaps we can frighten it away," suggested the wolves when the animals returned at dusk. They waited for the moon to come up, and then they howled and **HOWLED** and **HOWLED** at the Big Blue Thing.

HOOOWWWLLL

HOOOWWWLLL

Ho

But it did not move even one inch.

"Let us try," suggested the bears.
So they growled and **growled** and **GROWLED**
at the Big Blue Thing.

GRROOOWWLL   GRROOOWWLL

But it still did not
move even one inch.

GRROOOWWLL

"Perhaps we can nudge it back down the hill," suggested the boars.

They **huffed** and **puffed** as they **PUSHED** and **SHOVED** with all their might.

But the Big Blue Thing *still* didn't move, not even the tiniest bit.

"How about burying it?" suggested the foxes.
So the foxes, the badgers, and the weasels gathered around, and they **dug** and **dug** and then **DUG** some more.

But, just as it looked as though their plan might work…
the Big Blue Thing made a grumbling, **rumbling** noise.

"IT'S WAKING UP!" shouted the animals. And they all fled back to the safety of the Great Forest.

No one knew what to do next, so they called a general forest meeting to ask the Wise Owls what to do about the problem of the Big Blue Thing.

And after some **hoots** and **toots** and rather loud **WHOOPS,** the Wisest Old Owl announced a most clever plan.

The Wisest Old Owl explained:

" First, we summon the help of our **smallest** forest friends —
the bees and wasps, midges and skeeters — and we ask them
to form a **BIG BUG FLYING SQUAD.**

We could invite a snake or two along for good measure, too.

Then we wait until dawn.
When the Big Blue Thing starts to
wake up, the squad must go **inside**
the mouth of the beast, where they
must **whizz** and **buzz** and **BUZZ** and **whizz**
(and if necessary nip and sting).

Then it won't be long before that Big Blue Thing
is gone for good."

So, as the sun peeked
over the top of Howling Hill,
a **big** black cloud of the forest's finest bugs
(and a snake or two for good measure)
were ready to **ZOOM** in.

They **whizzed** and **buzzed**
as they flew and crawled through every crack,
right inside the Big Blue Thing.

It didn't take long before it was
clear that the Wisest Old Owl had been right!
With a **roar** and a **rumble**, the Big Blue Thing
turned tail and fled back down Howling Hill
and away to wherever it had come from.

And all the while, the animals screeched and GROWLED, roared and howled, snuffed and huffed, and generally made such a HULLABALOO that it was heard for miles and miles.

HOOOWWLL

HIIISSS

After that, things got back to normal
in the Great Forest at the foot of Howling Hill,
and every day was peaceful and
quiet ONCE MORE.

Until one fine night...